STEP INTO READING®

STEP 2

DISNEP
✦PRINCESS

A Pony
for a
Princess

By Andrea Posner-Sanchez

Illustrated by Francesc Mateu

Random House 🏠 New York

Belle picked out a book
from the castle library.

Then she looked
out the window.
The sun was shining.
"I think I will read
outside today," she said.

Belle left the castle.

She walked past the barn.

There was a big

pile of hay

by the barn.

She walked past
the apple tree.
There was a big
basket of apples
under the tree.

Belle sat down to read.

Belle read and read.
Before long,
she felt hungry.

Belle put down her book.
She walked back
to the castle
to get some lunch.

Belle put a sandwich, some lemonade, and some sugar cubes into a picnic basket.

"And I will pick
an apple for dessert,"
she said.

Belle went back outside.

She walked past the barn.

The hay was gone!

"That is odd," Belle said.

She walked past
the apple tree.
The basket was empty!

"Who could have
eaten all the apples?"
Belle asked.

Belle looked this way.

Belle looked that way.

Then she saw something

behind a bush.

It was a wild pony!

Belle stepped closer.

But the pony was scared.

It ran this way . . .

. . . and it ran that way.
But the pony would not
come to Belle.

Belle had an idea.

She took the sugar cubes

from the picnic basket.

She placed them in a row

on the grass.

Then she stepped back.

The pony ate one
sugar cube.

Then it ate another.
And another.

Soon the pony was
right next to Belle!

Belle held out the
last sugar cube.
The pony ate it right
from her hand!

She reached out to pat

the pony's soft nose.

Belle was happy.
She led the pretty pony
to the barn.

And before long,
the princess and
the pony became
great friends.